WHO WERE THE VIKINGS?

Jane Chisholm & Struan Reid

Illustrated by David Cuzik

Designed by Vicki Groombridge

Edited by Phil Roxbee Cox
History consultant: Anne Millard
Cover design: Russell Punter
Research assistant: Susanna Davidson

D0565538

CONTENTS

Who were the Vikings?

People who lived in Scandinavia (Sweden, Norway and Denmark) over a thousand years ago. They were fierce warriors and seafarers who attacked towns and villages all over Europe. The Vikings were hated and feared by their victims, which isn't at all surprising.

This is a statue of Leif Ericsson, a Norwegian Viking who was probably the first European to set foot in America.

Why didn't they just stay at home?

Good farmland was hard to find and there wasn't enough for everyone to have their own farm. Usually the eldest sons got all the land. Many raiders were landless younger sons who wanted to get rich quick.

Were they only savage warriors?

No. Many Vikings were farmers, craftspeople and traders. They were also great adventurers and explorers. Some went as far as Arabia and across the Atlantic Ocean to America.

Eric the Red, a Viking explorer, settled in Greenland after being expelled from Norway and Iceland.

ICELAND

NORWAY

SCOTLAND

SWEDEN

In 1066, England was conquered by Normans, who were descended from Vikings.

IRELAND

The city of Dublin was founded by Vikings.

Dublin

ATLANTIC OCEAN

ENGLAND

DENMARK

Irish treasure was looted by the Vikings.

The arrows show some of the places the Vikings went.

FRANCE

SPAIN

Normandy, in France, is named after Vikings (called Northmen, or Normans) who settled there.

ITALY

Mask of a Viking god

MEDITERRANEAN SEA

Silver cup

A Viking warrior carved from reindeer antler

2

These Vikings are pulling their longship through a Russian forest.

RUSSIA

The city of Novgorod, the capital of the first Russian state, was founded by Vikings.

River Volga

River Dnieper

Vladimir of Kiev, a Russian king descended from Viking settlers

Constantinople

BLACK SEA

Viking soldiers, like this one, worked for the Byzantine Emperor in Constantinople. They were called the Varangian guard.

BYZANTINE EMPIRE

What does 'Viking' mean?

Some experts believe it comes from the word *vikingr*, which means "pirate" or "raider" in Old Norse (the Viking language). Others think it may come from *vik*, meaning "bay".

Early Scandinavian church

When did the Viking age come to an end?

By about 1100. This was when Scandinavia was divided into the countries of Sweden, Norway and Denmark, each with its own king. The Vikings became Christians and began to lead a more settled way of life. Eventually there were no more raids.

CASPIAN SEA

Viking merchants went as far as Arabia to trade with the Arabs.

Baghdad

ARABIA

How do we know about the Vikings?

From the work of archaeologists. These are people who dig up old remains and study how people lived. Some accounts written at the time of the Vikings, usually by their victims, have also survived.

3

What did Vikings look like?

People often imagine Vikings as tall and fierce-looking, with long red beards and helmets with wings or horns on them. In fact, some Vikings may have been quite small, and their helmets were plain, with no horns.

What clothes did they wear?

Really warm ones. It was pretty cold most of the time. The women wore long dresses and the men wore trousers and tunics. These were usually made of wool or linen. They had thick cloaks of wool or fur.

A Viking frightening his enemies

Sword arm free in case of emergencies

Leather skullcap

Expensive tunic trimmed with Chinese silk

Cloak pinned on one shoulder

Headscarf

Viking chief

This merchant bought his fur hat and baggy trousers in Russia.

Tunic dress

Leather shoes

Did they really have big red beards?

Only the ones with red hair. And none of the women and children. Many Viking men did grow beards, probably to keep warm, look fierce and avoid shaving. But some of them would have had fair or even dark hair.

Loom

Weights

Where did they get their clothes?

The women made them at home. First they wove the material on a loom, using wool and linen threads (from a plant called flax). Then they sewed them and dyed them with dyes made from plants and rocks.

4

Were there Viking hairdressers?

No, but Vikings took great care over how they looked. Women wore their long hair tied back or in braids. The men often had long hair too, and sometimes braided their beards. This stopped the beards from blowing into their faces in the wind.

Some Viking hairstyles

This man is very pleased with his beard.

Do you know what these are?

Viking women didn't carry handbags. They hung the things they needed on a chain hanging from a brooch. Can you guess what each of the items is for? (You can find out on page 32.)

Did they paint their faces?

Yes, and not just the women. According to one visiting Arab trader, the men painted black powder called kohl around their eyes. Not to look pretty, but to appear even more frightening to their enemies.

Did they wear jewels?

Plenty of them. Both men and women wore rings and bracelets. Because they didn't use buttons they usually kept their clothes in place with belts and brooches.

Cloak pin

Necklaces

Silver bead

Carnelian bead

Glass beads

Brooch

Earrings

Bracelet

Rings

5

What was a Viking family like?

Very big and, if you were lucky, friendly too. Children, parents, grandparents, aunts, uncles and cousins all lived together in the same village – sometimes even in the same house. They all helped each other. Being loyal to the family was very important.

This swimmer is in trouble.

The chief of the village lives here.

These men have had a bad day's fishing.

Food shed

Pig sty

Hungry chickens

Animal shed

Where did they live?

On small farms mostly. Some Vikings didn't have a farm of their own. Instead they rented some land, or lived on another Viking's farm, in exchange for working for the chief.

The slaves all live in this hut.

Storage hut

Did the children go to school?

No. They didn't have lessons like reading and writing, but their parents taught them how to survive. When a boy was twelve, he was thought of as grown-up and had to look after himself.

What about the girls?

They learned how to spin, weave, cook and how to run the farm. When the men went off to fight, the women were left to look after the farm and protect it from attackers.

Building a new warship

Spear-throwing

Hungry ducks

These men are preparing to go raiding.

Sowing seeds

What did they grow?

Whatever they could. This included cereals like oats, barley, wheat and rye, and vegetables such as cabbages, onions, beans and peas, but no potatoes. They hadn't been discovered yet.

What animals did they keep?

The usual ones: pigs, sheep, goats, cattle, chickens, ducks and geese.

Blacksmith's workshop, where the blacksmith makes tools and weapons from iron

Chunks of iron ore are burned with charcoal in these clay irons. The fire melts them into iron.

It's hot and smoky here.

Back from a good day's hunting

Did they go hunting and fishing?

Yes, when they weren't farming or raiding. They hunted birds and large animals, such as elk, deer, wild boar (pig) and sometimes bear. They also went fishing, and hunted large sea animals such as walruses, seals, and even whales.

7

*Internet link: go to **www.usborne-quicklinks.com** for a link to a Web site where you can click on the buildings in a Viking village to find out what's going on inside.*

What were Viking houses like?

Long, usually. In fact, so long that they were called 'longhouses'. A longhouse was usually just one big room, where everyone ate, slept, worked and relaxed together. Only the chief and his wife sometimes had a room to themselves.

What were the houses made of?

Wood, mostly. The frame was built of strong wooden posts. The walls were made of logs, or woven wooden canes, plastered with mud to make them thicker and stronger. The roof was thatched with reeds or straw. There were no windows.

New grass turf roof

Hole for smoke

Stone foundations

This is a turf house from Greenland.

Were all the houses made like this?

No. In some places, such as Greenland, there weren't enough trees to make wooden houses. The Vikings built rather different houses there out of stone and turf (squares of grass and mud cut out of the ground). Thick turf helped keep the icy wind out.

Why didn't they have windows?

Because they would have let the cold in. This made it very dark inside. The only light came from the fire and from small clay lamps burning oil.

Woven wall-hanging

This is a Viking longhouse. The artist has cut away part of the roof so you can see inside.

This man is repairing a broken sword.

Loom for weaving

It's wild boar stew for supper again.

More wood for the fire

Internet link: go to **www.usborne-quicklinks.com** for a link to a Web site where you can play a game about what you would find in a Viking home.

Smoke hole

Did they have carpets and wallpaper?

No, the houses were much too simple for that. Sometimes they put rushes on the floor and hung animal skins or woven hangings on the wall. This all helped to keep the house warm.

Thatched roof

Some lucky animals are kept inside in winter.

This man loves wild boar stew. He's not waiting for the others.

Did they have toilets?

Yes, but they were in small huts outside. Not much fun on a cold winter's night. Inside the hut was a wooden seat over a bucket or a hole in the ground.

Toilet

Woven cane walls

These younger children are already asleep.

This boy is late with the pigs' supper.

What was Viking furniture like?

Probably not very comfortable. They didn't have much. People sat on benches and slept on platforms around the edge of the room. Only the chief and his wife slept in a bed. Can you spot one in the big picture? Blankets and clothes were kept in big chests.

A chief's bed

9

Did the Vikings believe in God?

They believed in many different gods and goddesses, who lived in a place called Asgard. The only way to reach Asgard was across a rainbow bridge called Bifrost. Vikings believed that their own world, called Midgard, was in the middle of a deep sea full of monsters.

Who was the most important god?

Odin. He was powerful and dangerous, as well as mysterious and wise. Odin could change into any bird or animal. Everyone was afraid of him.

Did they believe in the Devil?

No, but they believed in a naughty god called Loki. When things went wrong, people often blamed Loki. They also believed in wicked giants, dwarfs and dark elves.

Who were the giants and dwarfs?

The giants were evil creatures who often caused trouble. They lived in mountains across the sea from Midgard. The dwarfs were ugly and greedy, but very good at making things out of gold.

Odin

Mjollnir

Sleipnir, Odin's eight-legged horse

Thor

Which god did people like best?

Thor. He was big and jolly, with a bushy red beard and a booming laugh. People thought that thunder and lightning came from Thor riding his chariot across the skies.

Goats pulling Thor's chariot

Dwarfs

Loki

All these worlds are held together by the roots of a magic tree called Yggdrasil.

Giant

Frey

Freya

Asgard, where the gods live

Bifrost, the rainbow bridge

Who were the dark elves?

Funny little spirits who looked like little old men. If they were treated well, they were friendly. If not, they broke plates and caused trouble. They had their own enemies. They were always fighting the giants.

Did they believe in magic?

Yes. They thought there was good magic and bad magic. People called soothsayers cast spells and tried to use magic to see into the future.

Did they have temples or churches?

No, they worshipped their gods at home. On very special occasions, they held ceremonies outdoors in places called sacred groves.

Telling tales of magic around the fire

Chief leading ceremony

Food offerings for the gods

Statues of Viking gods

Midgard, where the Vikings live

Niflheim, an icy place. People went there when they died.

Did you know?

Thor carried a stone hammer that he used in his many battles with the troublesome giants. The hammer even had a name – *Mjollnir*. Many Vikings wore tiny hammer-shaped charms, called amulets, for good luck.

Amulets

What happened if they were ill?

They were looked after usually at home. If a warrior was wounded in battle, another warrior might help dress and bandage his wounds.

This Viking chief has been wounded in battle. He's really getting too old for fighting.

The women do most of the work, including brewing herbs to make potions.

Didn't they have doctors?

No, but some people knew all about making medicines from herbs and mending broken bones. Magic spells were expected to play a big part too.

The chief's brother is bandaging his arm. He has been wounded several times himself.

Medicine chest

Faithful hounds

Hot work

This boy is about to get into trouble.

This is the chief's sister. She looks very worried.

Her son looks more interested in his new puppy.

What happened if the person died?

This warrior broke his sword and shield in battle.

That depended on how important they were. Most people were just buried in a hole in the ground. Some warriors were burned on a pile of wood, called a pyre.

Food and drink

The body of a great chief or warrior was sometimes buried in a ship. The ship was then burned. People thought it would sail off to Valhalla, guided by Valkyries.

Grave of the dead chief's mother

Memorial stone marking a grave

Mourners

Treasure, weapons and other possessions

The chief's horse and one of his slave girls have been killed, so that they can go with him to Valhalla.

Some graves were marked with stones in the shape of a ship. This was less expensive than a proper ship burial.

What was Valhalla?

A little like heaven. This was where a warrior went when he died in battle. At night he would eat and drink with the gods. For a Viking this was a fun place.

Valhalla

Dead warrior

Valkyrie

Who or what were Valkyries?

Handmaidens of the god Odin. They swooped down out of the sky on white horses to carry off the souls of the warriors killed in battle.

What happened if a warrior didn't die in battle?

He would end up in Niflheim, where ordinary people went. This was an icy, misty place, with nothing much to do. To avoid this, some warriors even asked their friends to kill them! That way, they could go to Valhalla after all.

What was Viking food like?

Pretty boring probably. They could only eat what they could grow and hunt. The climate wasn't good enough for them to grow a great variety of food, and hunting was quite difficult in winter.

Wooden barrel

Drinking horn (the wrong way up)

Viking jugs and bowls

How do we know what they ate?

Because archaeologists have found seeds and animal and fish bones in Viking graves.

Viking vegetables

Garlic

Cabbage

Carrots

Berries

Hops for beer

Did they have parties?

Yes, on special occasions. After an enormous meal, musicians played harps and pipes and a professional poet, called a skald, recited poems – usually about the chief's daring deeds!

A little arm-wrestling

How did they manage in winter?

By eating meat and fish that had been packed in salt to preserve it. But this didn't help to make it taste very nice.

They eat with their fingers and a knife. They don't have forks.

Yet another fight!

They are drinking beer or mead (made from apples and honey).

Hunting in several feet of snow wouldn't have been much fun.

This dog is hoping for a goose for supper.

How did they cook the food?

Food could be grilled or spit-roasted over a fire, or baked in a hole in the ground packed with hot stones. Boiling or stewing was done by hanging a pot over the fire from a hook on the ceiling.

14

*Internet link: go to **www.usborne-quicklinks.com** for a link to a Web site which is packed with Viking recipes to try out.*

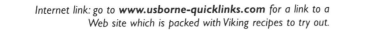

What was their music like?

Mostly harp or pipe music. We can only guess what it sounded like. Al-Tattushi, an Arab merchant, said the noise of Vikings singing was worse than howling dogs!

Did they drink a lot?

Yes, quite often. Some Viking raiders waited for people to get drunk before they attacked them. Then they couldn't defend themselves.

An enthusiastic toast

A drinking horn the right way up

This man has a headache.

Harpist harping

A skald reciting a poem

Piper piping

A thirsty drinker

Make Viking wild berry juice

Mash raspberries, blackberries or strawberries in a strainer over a bowl (to get the juice out). Then add water (about the same amount) and honey to taste.

What did the Vikings do for fun?

All sorts of things. When they weren't fighting, farming, hunting or house-keeping, they were enjoying themselves. They didn't have organized sports as we do, but if they got together for a special occasion, they often challenged each other to fights and competitions.

What sorts of competitions did they have?

Anything they were good at. Here are some of the different sports they played.

A stubborn pig

Wrestling

Whoever lands on the stone is the loser.

Swordfights could be quite dangerous, especially after a banquet when people had had a lot to drink.

This man finds weight-lifting very easy

The referee is here to make sure nobody cheats.

Chasing chickens

The man under the log isn't as strong as he thought.

A jump about to end in a bump

Did they have time off?

No, but they did celebrate three big religious festivals every year – at the beginning of summer, at harvest time and in the middle of winter. At each one, there were huge parties that went on for days.

Internet link: go to www.usborne-quicklinks.com for a link to a Web site where you can find out how some people think a Viking game called hnefatfl might have been played.

Smoked fish

Have you noticed two people who are crazy enough to take a dip in the icy water?

More food for the feast arriving on horseback

Guests arriving

Didn't they get bored in winter?

Yes. Playing board games and telling endless stories, called sagas, helped a little. Chess was popular, and so was something called *hnefatfl*. This may have been like chess. The rules have never been found, so nobody knows how to play it anymore.

These two have heard the story so often they'd rather play chess instead.

This storyteller is very popular.

What were the sagas about?

Gods and heroes, great adventures, battles, distant lands and strange people. Sagas were passed down from the oldest to the youngest in each family. Some were so long it took days to tell them.

Which saga did they like best?

Probably one with Thor in it. For a god, he wasn't very clever and kept on ending up in trouble. The ways he managed to escape were very exciting. There is a story about Thor on the next page.

Did you know?

Viking traders may have watched chess games in Arabia. They probably liked the game so much they brought the boards and pieces back home with them. Then, they would have taught the rules to their friends at home. Soon chess spread throughout the Viking lands.

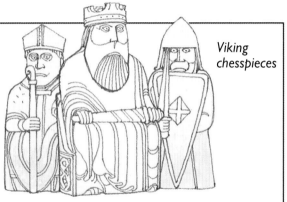

Viking chesspieces

17

There's more on the next page...

The night in the forest

Thor was the eldest son of Odin, king of the gods. He used his muscles when others would have used their wits. Thor loved a good battle or a trial of strength. In search of adventure, Thor decided to travel to Utgard, home of the giants. The giants were sworn enemies of the gods.

After a long day's travel, Thor and his fellow adventurers found themselves deep in the heart of a forest. In the gloomy twilight, they spotted the entrance to a strange building at the bottom of a small mountain. There was no door, just an enormous opening like the mouth of a cave.

Hammer raised, Thor strode into the building expecting a trap. He found himself in a huge hallway, with five open doorways leading off in different directions. When he challenged any enemies to come out and face him, his booming voice echoed into the darkness. The place was deserted.

Thor and his followers chose to sleep in the smallest of the rooms. They settled down for the night. It was not a peaceful one. More than once, they were awakened by what sounded like the roar of a thousand waterfalls, and the ground shaking like an earthquake.

At the crack of dawn, Thor strode out into the daylight. He could hardly believe his eyes. What he had thought to be a mountain was the body of a sleeping giant. The roaring and shaking had come from him snoring. Slowly, the god of thunder turned to look at the building in which he had spent the night. It was the giant's glove. The five 'rooms' were for the fingers. They had slept in the space for the thumb.

Could the Vikings read and write?

Only a few of them could, but stories, like the one about Thor, were passed on by word of mouth from generation to generation. The parents told them to their children, and they told them to their children. Sagas weren't written down until after the Viking age.

The Viking alphabet was called the futhark, after the first six letters: f, u, th, a, r, k.

What was Viking writing like?

It was made up of 16 letters, or marks, called runes. They didn't have enough runes for every sound in the Viking language. This made spelling very difficult. Can you write your name in Viking runes?

Reading from runes

These runes are carved on bone.

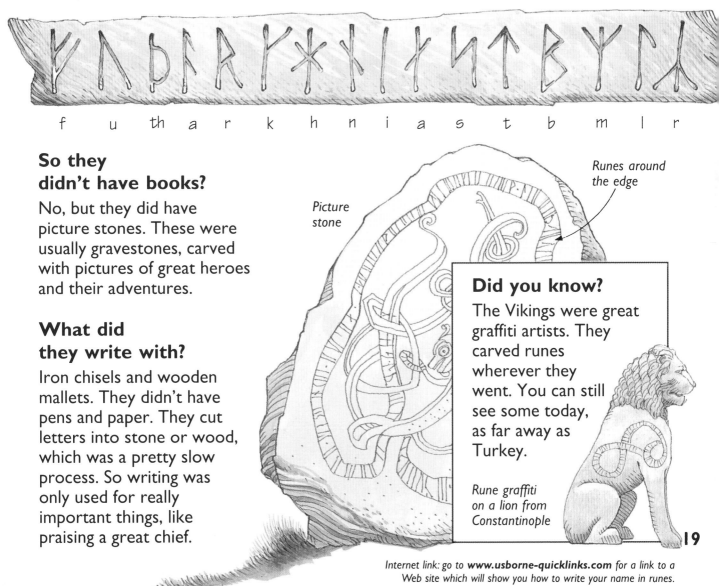

f u th a r k h n i a s t b m l r

So they didn't have books?

No, but they did have picture stones. These were usually gravestones, carved with pictures of great heroes and their adventures.

Picture stone

Runes around the edge

What did they write with?

Iron chisels and wooden mallets. They didn't have pens and paper. They cut letters into stone or wood, which was a pretty slow process. So writing was only used for really important things, like praising a great chief.

Did you know?

The Vikings were great graffiti artists. They carved runes wherever they went. You can still see some today, as far away as Turkey.

Rune graffiti on a lion from Constantinople

19

Internet link: go to www.usborne-quicklinks.com for a link to a Web site which will show you how to write your name in runes.

How did the Vikings get around?

By ships and boats, mostly. The Viking lands were covered with mountains, fjords, rivers, lakes and islands.

Vikings were all skilled sailors and shipbuilders. Thick forests provided plenty of wood for building boats.

Were there different types of boats?

Yes. Canoes, fishing boats, ferries, knorrs (trading ships) and, finest of all, the Viking warships. They were called longships, because they were so long, or dragon ships. Some longships had a dragon's head carved on the prow (front).

Dragon head

Prow

These people are building a longship.

Cross beams and ribs helped strengthen the hull (the ship's body).

Hitting the nail on the head

Tired boat-builder

Keel

A knorr *A fishing boat*

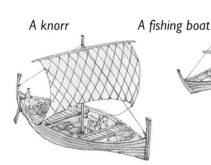

Long planks of wood, were very flexible in rough seas.

A picnic for the workers

Toolbox

Why did the Vikings carve dragons' heads on their ships?

To scare their enemies, of course. It must have looked frightening to see a pair of wild eyes and snarling teeth looming out of the fog.

A dragon's head prow

What was so special about longships?

They were so fast they cut through the water like knives. They were also very strong, but still light enough to be carried if necessary. They were very shallow.

*Internet link: go to **www.usborne-quicklinks.com***
for a link to a Web site where you can try sailing a
Viking longship from Greenland to Newfoundland.

You'll find he fell off his ladder on page 7 too.

Stern

Oars

Nailing a finger

Tar

Iron rivets

This holds up the mast, sail and oars.

Why were their ships so shallow?

So they could sail quickly and quietly up shallow rivers. Even when the longships were packed with warriors, they could take a village completely by surprise.

Who built them, and how?

Professional ship-builders, but the whole village might join in. There was probably a shipyard attached to most big villages. The best ships were made of oak, but pine and birch were also used.

How did they travel in winter?

If the lakes and rivers were frozen over, people got around on skis, ice skates and horse-drawn sleighs. But they didn't travel much in winter.

How do we know about Viking ships?

Because some of the ships that were buried have actually survived, even though they are over a thousand years old. The soil stopped the wood from rotting away.

The remains of a Viking ship

21

Did the Vikings go shopping?

Not often. Most Vikings lived in the country and grew and made the things they needed for themselves. There were shops and markets in the towns, though. Merchants and craftspeople journeyed long distances to reach them.

What was it like in a Viking town?

Crowded and smoky from all the fires in people's houses. Most towns were by the sea, or on the edge of a river, so people could arrive by boat.

Farm animals live in the town too.

Weavers

The lookout on the lookout

Weary merchants bringing goods to market

Wooden walkways

Repairing the roof

Slave market

Fur trader

What kinds of crafts did people make?

Fishmonger smoking his fish

Leatherworkers made shoes and boots. Bronze and silversmiths made necklaces, brooches and dishes. Bone carvers made pins and combs from deer antlers. Blacksmiths made tools and weapons.

Boatyard

If you look very carefully, you can just about make out some of these

22 people at work.

Boat ramp

Internet link: go to **www.usborne-quicklinks.com** for a link to a Web site where you can go shopping in a Viking town.

This house isn't supposed to be burning down.

What Viking goods could you buy?

Honey, wax, furs, glass, cloth, walrus ivory, swords, slaves and treasures made from silver and precious stones. Some of these things were probably stolen on raiding expeditions.

What foreign goods were for sale?

Gold and silver coins from Arabia, wheat from England, wine from the Mediterranean, silks and spices from the East, and amber from the Baltic Sea.

Sheep

Pigs

Pottery

Blacksmiths lived on the edge of the town. This helped to prevent the whole town from burning down if a fire broke out.

Foreign treasures

Did they use money?

At first, they just exchanged things, or paid with silver, jewels or coins they had brought back from abroad. By the 10th century though, Vikings were making their own coins.

Early Viking coins

Arab merchants selling silk

This ship is loaded up for the journey home.

Wine merchant

23

Did the Vikings have kings?

Yes, plenty of them. All at once. As time went on, there were fewer kings, but the ones that were left had more land and power. In the end, there were just three – one each for Denmark, Sweden and Norway.

How much power did the early kings have?

Probably not as much as they would have liked. But they were more important than the jarls and karls.

A king

What were jarls?

The richest, most important chiefs. They owned lots of land and employed other Viking warriors.

A jarl

Who were the karls?

Free men and women. Karls could fight and own their own land, and the men could vote at the Thing.

A karl

Wasn't everyone free?

The slaves, or thralls, weren't. They had a pretty tough time, working hard for no pay. Thralls could be bought and sold for a few furs or a barrel of wine.

24 *A thrall*

What's a Thing?

An open-air meeting, where Vikings met to discuss local problems, settle arguments and punish criminals. Things were held only every two or three years, but they lasted for days. People took them very seriously.

This thief has been sent away forever.

These women are enjoying a chat before supper.

His family is very sad to see him go.

This man is being tried for stealing horses.

These people are late. They were so busy raiding, they forgot about the Thing.

A thief hoping to steal a horse

Three chiefs have been chosen to act as judges.

A man called the lawspeaker recites the law to the crowd.

When the business is over, everyone enjoys themselves. These people are watching a horse-fight.

This quarrel is being settled by a duel.

How did they settle arguments?

Usually the judges decided who was in the right and who was in the wrong. But if they really couldn't make up their minds, they might try to ask the gods.

This man is being made to walk on hot stones. The Vikings believe that, if he is innocent, the gods will stop his feet burning. This is called "trial by ordeal".

What kinds of punishments did they have?

A criminal could be outlawed (sent away forever), fined, made a slave or, in extreme cases, put to death. Rich people got bigger fines.

Did they have an army?

Not exactly, but all Viking men learned how to fight and use weapons from an early age. They needed these skills to make them successful raiders. They also had to defend their homes and fight off pirates.

What weapons did they use?

Swords for stabbing people, and axes with huge blades for chopping peoples' heads off. They were very proud of their weapons, and even gave them names like *Skull-splitter*, *Leg-biter* and *the Adder*.

Wooden shield covered in leather

Padded leather jacket

Viking warriors ready for battle

Sword

This man's axe is called "Dragon-slayer".

What did they wear to protect themselves?

Not much. One very strange group of warriors, called the beserks, even fought without any protection. People thought they must have magic powers. When the beserks were around, everyone was scared – even other Vikings!

This shirt, made of thousands of iron rings, is called a byrnie. Most people can't afford this.

A brave priest

Weren't people frightened of them?

Yes, absolutely terrified. The Vikings were the most feared warriors of their time. People called them "the terror of the North".

This decorated sword probably belonged to a Viking chief.

This fine helmet is made of copper and leather. Notice that it doesn't have any horns or wings on it.

These people may be lucky enough to escape.

Where did they go raiding?

All over Europe – from Germany, Britain and Ireland, around the coasts of France and Spain as far as Italy.

These are the raiders who were late for the Thing on page 25.

These raiders have found a good store of treasure in the church.

These women are going to be carried off as slaves.

This woman knows how to use a broom.

Did they ride into battle?

Some of the chiefs did, but most warriors couldn't afford a horse. Instead they ran into battle, waving their weapons, and screaming at their terrified victims.

Did you know?

Vikings sometimes buried their treasure in hoards. Archaeologists have found so many of these, it looks as if some people forgot where they had buried things, or died before they could dig them up.

Decorated box found in a hoard

Were all the Vikings ruthless raiders?

Not at all, but the raiders gave them a bad name. Viking merchants went abroad for trading, not raiding. Other Vikings went looking for a place to live.

SWEDEN

RUSSIA

Viking routes

Constantinople

Baghdad

MEDITERRANEAN SEA

Where did Viking traders go?

All over Europe, north and west to Iceland and Greenland, south down the Russian rivers as far as the rich city of Constantinople (now Istanbul in Turkey), and across deserts to the Arabian city of Baghdad (now in Iraq).

This is a busy market in Constantinople.

A small disagreement

Beer for thirsty shoppers

An Arab trader

Scales for weighing metals

This man is sure he is being cheated. But he isn't.

Unlucky slave girls for sale

A proud carpet seller from Persia

This man's customers have come all the way from China.

These men are carrying the mast separately.

Hauling the boat overland

Did they really go all that way by boat?

No. Some of the rivers had dangerous rapids, and some of the routes went overland. Then they had to carry their boats to the next river, by hauling them along the ground on logs.

Internet link: go to www.usborne-quicklinks.com for a link to a Web site where you can find out more about Viking trade, travel and exploration and enter a quiz called Thorkel's challenge.

Were the Vikings good craftsmen and women?

Yes, they made beautiful things, carved in wood, bone, gold and silver. Viking designs look like a lot of swirling lines. If you look closely, you can often see that these are really animals and monsters gripping on to each other.

Decorated bronze part of a horse harness

Gold pendant

Silver brooch

Woodcarver at work

This sort of design is known as a 'gripping beast'.

Why did they decorate things with pictures of monsters?

Because Vikings believed the seas and skies were full of them, often with magical powers. By carving monsters on things, they thought they could protect themselves from danger.

Sharp swords and knives from France

Did you know?

Russia is actually named after a Viking tribe called the Rus. This is because the first ever kingdom in Russia was set up in the 9th century by a Rus man called Rurik.

Russian style Viking silver

How far did Viking settlers go?

A long way. There were Viking settlements in Russia, France, Britain, Ireland, Iceland, Greenland and even North America.

GREENLAND

BRITAIN

ICELAND

Newfoundland

ATLANTIC OCEAN

NORTH AMERICA

The red parts show Viking settlements.

What was it like on board ship?

Cold, wet and very uncomfortable. In a storm it would have been pretty frightening too. Crossing the ocean was much slower in those days.

How did they find their way?

With difficulty. Although they had years of experience, they had no instruments to guide them – only the sun and stars. Sometimes they followed flocks of birds and shoals of fish.

Amazing Viking bird monster

Seabirds flying south for winter

Beards flying in the wind

Barrels of food and drink for the trip

This chicken has had enough.

Camping things

Fresh water

Sea water

The type of boat is called a knorr. It is wider, deeper and slower than a longship.

Did you know?

The picture on the left is of a bronze weather vane from a Viking ship. Streamers were attached to tiny holes along the bottom. These would rattle and blow in the wind, showing the sailors where the wind was coming from.

Stormy weather

A Viking settlement in Greenland

A damaged sail

Turf roofs

Did they stay long?

Not in America. The native Americans weren't very friendly and there were fights and raids. Also, there were too few Vikings to build a successful settlement. Eventually, they were forced to leave. They had more luck in Iceland and Greenland though.

These horses and pigs aren't very happy.

These people are wishing they'd stayed at home.

The Vikings would have called this man a skraeling (meaning "wretch"). He is actually a native American.

Was Greenland very green?

No, but it wasn't quite as icy and cold as it is today. Eric the Red, who discovered the island, just called it Greenland to make it sound like a nice place to live. He wanted other Vikings to come and live there too.

Bags of seed for sowing crops

Did you know?

A Norman ship

William the Conqueror was descended from a group of Vikings who settled in northern France. They took control of the area, which was named Normandy (the land of the Northmen) after them.

31

Internet link: go to **www.usborne-quicklinks.com** for a link to a Web site where you can test your Viking knowledge with an interactive quiz.

Index

Answers

Page 5
The items are:
a key, a needle, a pair
of tweezers.

First published in 1995 by Usborne Publishing Ltd,
83-85 Saffron Hill, London EC1N 8RT, England.
www.usborne.com. Copyright © 2002, 1995
Usborne Publishing Ltd. The name Usborne and
the devices ⚇ ⚇ are Trade Marks of Usborne
Publishing Ltd. All rights reserved. No part of this
publication may be reproduced, stored in a
retrieval system, or transmitted in any form or by
any means, electronic, mechanical, photocopying,
recording or otherwise, without the prior
permission of the publisher. Printed in Belgium.
First published in the U.S. in 1995